STRANGE
MONSTER
STORIES

by
D. J. Arneson

A Watermill Press Book

TABLE OF CONTENTS

Cover Art — West & Wohler Associates, Inc.

ISBN 0-89375-221-5

Copyright 1979 DJArneson/Andor Publishing Inc.

184 Central Ave., Old Tappan, N.J. 07675

Produced by JRS Inc. All rights reserved.

Except for use in a review the reproduction of this work in whole or part by any means now known or ever invented is forbidden without the permission of the publisher.

The Sky Demon

"Eagle Leader to Eagle Squadron."

The three F-15 pilots listened to their squadron leader over the radio.

"We're 20 minutes from base. Begin descent now."

The four pilots dipped the noses of their planes toward the earth. Far ahead was their base.

"Eagle Leader, this is Eagle 3," Major Bill Donavan said.

"Roger, Eagle 3."

Bill Donavan looked out the cockpit of his sleek jet. A thick thunderhead loomed in front of the flight.

"That looks like a nasty one, Eagle leader. Do you want us to punch through or go around?"

The radios in the three planes following the leader crackled.

"Punch a hole through it, guys. It's big but it's not mean."

"Roger," Major Donavan replied.

The other two pilots also acknowledged the call.

The planes held a steady course. The cloud towered above them. They were at 30,000 feet. The cloud rose another 30,000.

"Looks bigger than I thought," Lt. Colonel Dusty Rhodes, the group leader, radioed as the planes neared the edge of the mammoth cloud.

"Must go to at least 60,000" Hank Walters said. Hank was a Lieutenant. He was the lowest ranking pilot. He flew aircraft number four. He would be the last to enter the cloud.

"At least," Captain Jeff Spriggs replied.

All four pilots watched as the cloud grew even taller. It was miles wide. The edges were snowy white but deep inside, dark gray billows were turning black. The cloud was directly in their path. Base was just on the other side.

"Want to go around?" Donavan called.

"Negative," their leader answered.

The jets, speeding through the sky at over 500 miles per hour would be through the cloud in less than a minute. To go around would consume time. More importantly, the delay would waste fuel.

The planes looked like toys against the massive cloud. A farmer on the ground who heard the planes looked up. He saw the four tiny aircraft plunge into the cloud. One by one they disappeared. The farmer took off his straw hat and wiped his brow with the back of his arm.

Lieutenant Walters' plane was the last to enter.

Instantly the sky and the earth vanished. There was nothing outside the cockpit but inpenetrable white. Even the wingtips were invisible. Lieutenant Walters lowered his head. He kept his eyes glued on his instruments. His steady hands kept the plane on course.

"Right behind you, Eagle three," he called on the radio. "Tell me when you break out."

There was no reply.

Walters pressed the mike button again. "Eagle leader? This is Eagle four. Let me know when you get out of this stuff, O.K.? It's thicker than the wool on a sheep's back in December." Walters grinned. He liked using phrases that described things the way he felt. Military terms were sometimes too stiff for him.

The radio remained silent.

"Eagle leader. Do you copy?"

There was complete silence.

A shadow passed over the cockpit. Hank Walters jerked his head up automatically.

"AAAaaaaaaaaahhhhhhhhhhh!"

Eagle 4 broke out of the boiling cloud. Two young boys on bikes heard the jet. They looked up. They saw a single shiny fighter zip out of the odd cloud.

"That's what I want to be when I grow up," one of the boys said.
"Me too," the other replied.

Neither boy knew that there should have been four airplanes in the clear blue sky above their heads, not just one.

Sergeant Clifford Robinson hurried to Eagle four as it taxied to a stop. Sergeant Robinson was Hank Walters' ground crew chief.

Sergeant Robinson scampered up the yellow ladder he had wheeled into place next to the parked aircraft. He looked in at his friend. He couldn't believe his eyes. Lieutenant Walters face was as gray as fried liver. He sat in the plane staring out.

"Lieutenant!" Sergeant Robinson shouted as the canopy opened.

The young flight officer didn't move.

Robinson reached in and removed the pilot's helmet. "What happened to the others . . . ?"

Robinson's jaw dropped open.

Lieutenant Walters' hair was as white as snow. The ruddy, red-faced young officer with the sandy brown hair was as colorless as notebook paper.

It was a full three days before Hank Walters was able to speak. Six doctors surrounded his hospital bed. With them was General Mark Andrews.

"Please tell General Andrews what you told us, Lieutenant," the head doctor said.

Hank blinked his eyes in the light. He turned slowly toward the general.

"It ate them," he muttered.

General Mark Andrews leaned forward. "*What* did he say?"

"Speak louder, Hank," one of the doctors said.

Hank's mouth moved slowly.

"The . . . thing . . . ate them."

General Andrews shook his head. He signalled the doctors to step outside.

In the hall the men whispered to one another.

"It's clear he has had a serious fright," one of the doctors said.

"The disappearance of the other planes has caused him to feel guilty."

"Why is that?" General Andrews asked.

"He survived," the doctor answered. "He feels he should

have been lost and that the others should have survived instead of him."

"Commendable," the General said, "But feeling guilty will not bring the others back." He scratched his head, "Or explain what happened," he added.

They entered Hank's room again.

"Now, Hank," the General said in a pleasant, friendly voice, "I realize you feel bad that your comrades have vanished. However, we must try to learn why. You must tell us what happened.

Hank pulled himself upright. He looked at the doctors. He looked at General Andrews.

"It's true," he said, "I entered the cloud right behind the others. I went on instruments immediately. About one minute into the cloud I called for Eagle three. I asked him to tell me when he broke out of the clouds. He didn't answer. I called for Eagle leader. He didn't answer. Nobody answered." His face was showing signs of fear. "Suddenly a dark cloud seemed to pass over my plane. The cockpit became instantly dark. I looked up . . ." He swallowed hard. He had trouble talking. "I looked up and I saw . . ." His eyes grew large. His mouth became dry. He raised his hands to cover his face.

"AAAaaaaaaaahhhh!"

The doctors went quickly to his side. Soon he was sleeping.

"Hmm," General Andrews wondered, "Something is preventing him from telling the truth."

The doctors listened.

"My guess is that an accident occured. Perhaps Walters was to blame. Perhaps not. But he refuses to tell us. Perhaps he is trying to protect whoever caused the accident.

The doctors nodded. None of them could come up with a better answer.

A week later Lieutenant Walters was discharged from the base hospital. He was restricted to the base. He was not allowed to fly. An investigation into the accident was begun.

Sergeant Robinson knocked on Lieutenant Walters' door.

"Who is it?" Walters asked.

"It's me, Lieutenant, Sergeant Robinson."

Walters opened the door. "Am I glad to see a friend, Clifford."

The two men shook hands.

"I heard about the investigation, Lieutenant," Sergeant Robinson said. "I have something I want to show you."

"What is it?" Hank asked anxiously.

"I don't know. That's why I think you should see it," the Sergeant replied.

The two men walked to the air field. They went directly to the hanger where Lieutenant Walters' plane was being held. It was evidence for the investigation. Nobody else was allowed to fly it until the mysterious disappearance of its three mates was solved.

Sergeant Robinson rolled the ladder up to the gleaming fuselage. He pointed. Hank Walters climbed the ladder. Clifford Robinson was right behind.

"What did you find?" Lieutenant Walters asked. He was very nervous. He hadn't been near his airplane since it landed on that fateful day.

The sergeant took Hank Walters' hand and brushed it against the skin of the aircraft. A deep frown crossed the Lieutenant's brow. He rubbed his fingers over the side of the plane which his crew chief had pointed out.

"Deep scratches!" he said.

Robinson nodded.

"Ten of them. A perfect row!" he said. Then he pointed to another section of the airplane's body. There was another identical set of deep scratch marks.

"What are they?" Hank Walters asked.

"I don't know, Lieutenant," the sergeant said. "But they weren't there when you went up that day. I went over this ship myself. Every inch."

"When did you find them?" the anxious young officer asked.

"Right after I helped you out of the cockpit that day!"

Walters shuddered.

"Whatever made those scratch marks made them up there." The sergeant pointed up into the sky.

"Then you believe my story?" the lieutenant asked.

"I believe something happened, Lieutenant," the crew chief responded. "And I believe you know what it was."

Lieutenant Walters put his arm on his crew chief's shoulder. "Thank you, Clifford. The rest of them are saying I'm crazy."

The sergeant smiled. "I did too," he said, "But when I remembered those scratch marks, I knew you were telling the truth."

Both men turned to look at the peculiar marks.

"You said it tried to grab you with its claws," Sergeant Robinson said, "And those claw marks are the proof."

"It was monstrous," the Lieutenant said, relieved that he could now tell his story to someone who knew he wasn't crazy. "I saw the black shadow. I thought maybe one of the other planes had dropped back. I looked up." Lieutenant Walters swallowed hard. He forced himself to speak. "There was a clearing in the center of the cloud. I saw the other planes. I saw the . . . the creature. It was at least a thousand feet tall. It had huge wings. Its mouth was as large as a tunnel. It was open wide. The other planes flew straight in. They hadn't seen it in time . . ."

The nervous Lieutenant leaned on the ladder. Sergeant Robinson held out his hand to support his friend.

"They vanished inside the thing. I was right behind them. I pulled back on the stick. I turned just in time. I banked away. I started to dive. The thing reached out for me. I saw those giant claws grabbing for me..." He stopped. Perspiration was pouring from his forehead. He was shaky. "The next thing I remember is waking up in the hospital."

Sergeant Robinson put his hand on the deep claw marks again. He rubbed them. They had gouged the metal but had slipped off before they could close around the fleeing plane.

Lieutenant Walters walked to the hanger door. He looked up into the sky.

"Sergeant!"

Sergeant Robinson raced to the huge doorway. He looked up into the sky. The mammoth cloud was back. It was the same one. There was no doubt in his mind. He had seen it the first day.

Walters grabbed the crew chief by the arm. "I'm going up," he shouted. The crew chief ran to the plane. It would be ready by the time the lieutenant got into his flight suit.

The engine boomed. Hot gases poured out the rear. It rolled toward the flight line.

Lieutenant Walters called the tower for permission to take off. There was a flurry of excited talk in the tower.

"Negative, Eagle four. You are restricted."

Lieutenant Walters looked up into the sky. A squadron of F-15's was approaching. They were from the base. They were pilots he knew. If they flew into the cloud, the thing would get them.

Walters shoved the throttle forward. The sleek jet began to roll.

He gave the craft full throttle. It shot down the runway. It was airborne.

Lieutenant Walters pointed the nose of his plane at the billowing giant cloud.

"Condor flight leader, this is Eagle four. Break off immediately. Do not penetrate the thunderhead."

"Who is this?" Hank Walters radio squawked.

"This is Lieutenant Hank Walters . . ."

There was silence.

"I know what you're thinking," Walters shouted. "Trust me. Don't enter that cloud!"

The four jets peeled away. They skimmed by the edge of the cloud.

Hank Walters flew directly into the towering cloud. Instantly everything vanished. He could not see a thing. Suddenly he was in the clear. He snapped his head around.

The thing was above him. It swooped down on its massive fluttering wings. Its talons glistened like giant steel spikes.

Hank Walters yanked back the stick. The aircraft snapped around. It was flying directly at the creature, heading right toward its huge, open mouth.

Lieutenant Walters waited. When the creature loomed so large in front of him that it blocked out everything else, he pressed the trigger on the control stick. No missiles launched. No tracer bullets streaked the sky. His plane was unarmed.

Late that afternoon General Mark Andrews and his staff gathered in a darkened room. The doctors were also there. Lieutenant Hank Walters stood by a motion picture screen. A projector began to roll.

On the screen was the creature. It loomed larger and larger. General Andrews gasped for breath just as the creature disappeared. The agile jet had turned away at the last minute.

The men sat in silence.

"It's still up there," General Andrews said at last.

Lieutenant Hank Walters slowly nodded his head.

"It's still up there," he said.

The Living Spine

Marvin Merton chuckled to himself. His uncle, kindly old Doc Merton was dead at last. Marvin had tricked his uncle into signing a false will. The false will left all of Doc Merton's possessions to Marvin.

"Heh, heh," Marvin laughed. "What he didn't know can't hurt him now."

Marvin was in his uncle's old office. The office was closed. All of Doc Merton's patients were gone. The nurse was gone. There was nothing left but three rooms of furniture. There were some boxes of medical things and some filing cabinets. And there were two closets full of junk.

Marvin poked around the office. "None of this stuff is worth anything," he said. He rubbed his hands together. "But what do I care? I've got the property in Oklahoma. I'm sure there's oil on it. I'll be rich." He looked at a picture of Doc Merton's wife on the doctor's well-worn desk. "Too bad, Aunt Fanny. You don't get anything." He tossed the picture on the pile of junk to be thrown out. The garbage truck would come by later to take everything to the dump.

Later that day Marvin sat at the desk. He was writing figures on a sheet of paper. He threw his pen down. "Drat! The stuff in this office isn't worth the money to have it hauled to the dump," he grumbled. He looked at the heap of old things on the floor. "I'll save the money and dump it myself."

Marvin loaded box after box of Doc's things into his van. It was soon loaded to the roof. He went back into the office for a last look around.

Marvin poked his head into each room. They were stripped bare. The few things of value he had put on the seat of his van. Now the rooms were empty.

Marvin put his hand on the office door to close it for the last time.

"Whoops!" he said. He walked to a small closet. "I forgot this closet," he muttered, "I hope it's empty. I'm tired of going through the old codger's collection of junk."

The closet door opened with a squeak. It was dark inside. Marvin poked his head in. "What's this?" he asked. He felt inside with a hand. "Ouch!" he pulled his hand back as if he had been stung. A tiny drop of blood formed on his finger. He licked it with his tongue.

Marvin lit a match. He held it inside the closet. "Yi!" he exclaimed. He jumped back. The match went out. He grinned. "You got yourself spooked, didn't you?" he asked himself. He lit another match. He put his head into the closet again.

Hanging from a wire in the corner of the closet was a long gray object. It was a human spine. It was a backbone that Doc Merton used to demonstrate ailments to his patients. He was a thorough doctor, who wanted his patients to understand their problems.

Marvin pulled the spine from its hanger. It was very old. It was covered with dust. The small wires which held it together squeaked when Marvin flexed the spine. One small wire jutted out. It was the wire that had pricked Marvin's finger.

Marvin studied the long chain of connected bones. It was an amazing thing. It was as flexible as a slinky toy but could be as stiff as a board. But Marvin wasn't interested in such things. All he cared about was his Uncle's money and property. Once the office was rented he could go to Oklahoma. He would sell the land for a tidy profit.

Marvin carried the floppy old bone spine to the van. He tossed it in the back on the pile of junk. He got behind the wheel. He waved goodbye at the office. "So long, sucker," he said, as if his old uncle could hear. He drove to the dump.

"That's the end of "Good Old Doc Merton"," he scoffed as he tossed the last of the doctor's possessions into the dump. "Good riddance to bad rubbish." Marvin went to close the van door. "You again," he growled. The spine was lying in the corner, on the floor, almost out of sight.

Marvin grabbed it. "Ouch!" he hollered. Again a drop of blood appeared on the end of his finger. He grabbed the spine and shook it. "I ought to smash you to pieces," he said. "I ought to take you apart bone by bone." He was very upset. He spun the spine around and around above his head. He let go. It sailed far over the trash heap. It landed out of sight near a pile of stinking garbage. "I hope you like your new home," he laughed. He got into his van and drove away.

Late that night the moon rose over the dump. A thousand rats scurried through the darkness looking for food. Bats skimmed low over the garbage, snapping insects out of the air. Giant bullfrogs croaked noisily from a swamp near the dump.

A moonbeam cut through the darkness. It touched the spine. The spine began to glow. It began to wiggle. It began to move!

A rat gnawing on a rotten pumpkin stopped gnawing. Others running by stopped in their tracks. The spine began to bend and flex. It curved and wiggled. It began to glide over the ground like a snake.

Marvin sat in his room. He studied the will his uncle had signed. "Everything is mine," he gloated. "And tomorrow I will be in Oklahoma." He went to the window. It was dark out. The only light came from the pale moon. His van sat in the shadows on the street. "By next week I'll be rich," he boasted. As he turned his head, something on the street caught his eye. He looked down through the darkness.

"What is that?" he wondered.

A thin reflection glowed in the shadow of his van. He looked up at the moon. "The moon must be reflecting off of something," he said. He blinked his eyes. The reflection moved. He could see a pale, S-shape on the ground next to his van. "Must be a rope or something," he said. He closed the window. He locked it. He pulled the shade.

A short time later Marvin was ready for bed. He looked at himself in the mirror as he brushed his teeth. "You fooled the old guy good," he said. "Aunt Fanny will never know there's a real will around. She'll never know she was supposed to get everything . . ."

He stopped. He cocked his head toward the door.

A rustling sound greeted his ears.

Marvin walked slowly to the door. The door was rattling softly. It was as if somebody was testing the handle. Marvin put his hand on the handle. It was jiggling. He pulled his hand back.

The door was locked.

"Who's there?" he asked through the door.

There was no answer.

"Is someone out there?"

Again there was no answer.

Marvin listened. Whatever it was, was moving. He looked at the floor. A shadow moved across the sliver of light coming from under the door.

Marvin began to sweat. He swallowed with a loud gulp. The handle began to jiggle again. He watched as the handle turned and turned. It turned past the point it should have stopped. Something was twisting the handle right off the door.

POP!

The handle popped off the door. It rattled on the floor at Marvin's feet. Marvin stared at the hole where the handle had been. A long gray object poked through the hole.

Marvin's eyes bugged open wide.

The thing began to twist and turn. It wriggled through the hole. It drilled the hole larger and larger by twisting around and around.

With a final crunching sound the spine shot out of the hole and flew through the air. It wrapped around Marvin's leg.

"Aaaaaaiiiiieeeee!" Marvin screamed.

The spine wriggled up his leg.

Marvin grabbed the twisting, turning thing in his hands. He tugged at it. He pulled. But he could not break its grip.

"Get off of me!" he screamed. But the glowing chain of bones climbed higher and higher. It reached the struggling man's waist. It wrapped around him like a belt.

Marvin forced his hands under the thing. He pulled with all of his might. He pulled the spine loose. Marvin pitched it across the room. The spine fell to the floor.

Marvin stared at it. Slowly the linked old gray bones began to wiggle. The spine shook itself. Then it slithered across the floor toward Marvin.

Marvin grabbed a lamp. He hurled it at the spine. The lamp shattered but the spine kept crawling, crawling, crawling.

Marvin leaped on top of his couch. The spine coiled on the floor. It shuddered. Then it leaped high into the air. It whipped its tail end around Marvin's neck. It wrapped itself around his head. It covered his eyes. It began to squeeze, squeeze, squeeze.

"Help me! Somebody help me!" Marvin pleaded.

The spine held tight. It would not let go.

Marvin fell against his desk. The drawer slid open. A sheet of paper fluttered to the floor. It was the real will.

Marvin clawed the spine from his eyes. He peered out from behind the coil of connected bone. He spotted the will.

"Aunt Fanny!" he screamed. "Help me, Aunt Fanny. You can have the will. You can have everything."

The spine loosened its grip.

Marvin gasped for air. The thing still clung to his neck.

"I promise. I'll call her right now. Just let me go. I'll tell her about the will . . . I'll tell her everything." Marvin was pleading for his life. For the first time in his life he was telling the truth.

The spine dropped to the floor. It curled into a coil, ready to spring at the first wrong move.

Marvin called his aunt. He kept one eye on the vibrating spine. When he had told his aunt the whole truth he covered his eyes with his hands. When he took them away the spine was gone.

Marvin never saw the spine again. Nobody ever saw the spine again. But Marvin knows its out there, watching and waiting. He does not know when or where it will strike next.

Or who!

The Thing In The Grate

Bud Klee sat nervously at his desk. Miss Harrow, his History teacher was writing on the board.

"These are the test questions, class", Miss Harrow said. "Write the answers to your questions on a clean sheet of paper. When you are finished, raise your hand."

Miss Harrow looked at her watch. She looked at the clock on the wall. "You will have 15 minutes. Begin!"

Bud wiggled in his seat. He had not studied for the test. He wasn't a very good student to begin with. He stared at the blank sheet of paper on his desk. There was no way he could fill it with answers. He did not have any.

Miss Harrow looked across the room. All her students were busy writing. Her eyes stopped on Bud. He was not writing. He was not doing anything.

Miss Harrow walked softly to Bud's desk:

"Is something wrong, Bud?" she asked.

Bud gulped. He nodded his head.

"What is it, Bud?" Miss Harrow said.

"I don't know the an . . . "

Bud stopped. His eyes had wandered to the air-conditioning grate in the wall. It was just a few feet above his head.

"Yes, Bud, I'm waiting," Miss Harrow said.

"Um, er, I was just thinking, that's all," Bud answered quickly. He spoke to Miss Harrow but he didn't take his eyes off the grate.

"Well, you'd better think fast," Miss Harrow said, looking at her watch. "Time is running out." She went back to her desk.

Bud looked around the room. Everyone was bent over their test paper. He turned his head slowly. He stared at the grate.

A pair of huge eyes stared back!

Bud gulped. He blinked his eyes. The eyes in the grate blinked back.

Bud raised his right hand slowly. He did not want to attract Miss Harrow's attention. He wiggled his fingers in a tiny wave at the grate.

A bony-looking hand inside the grate wiggled its fingers back.

Bud held up three fingers.

The hand in the grate held up three fingers.

Bud closed one eye.

The thing in the grate closed one eye.

"Bud? What are you doing?" Miss Harrow was standing by Bud's desk again.

Bud rubbed his eye. "I, uh, I got something in my eye," he said.

Miss Harrow looked at his blank paper. "Well, you'd better get something on your paper soon or you'll really have something to blink about," she said. She returned to her desk.

Bud shrugged his shoulders at the thing in the grate. He began to form words with his mouth without speaking them. "I'm stuck," he formed.

The thing in the grate began to move its mouth. It was hard to see because the grate was in the way.

"I can't see what you're saying," Bud mouthed.

"Bzz bzz sst bzt sssss", the thing in the grate whispered.

Bud smiled a smile so wide it hurt his jaw.

He grabbed his pencil. He wrote a bold number 1 on his test paper. He looked up at the board. He frowned. He studied the question.

"What was the name of the ship the Pilgrims came to the New World on?" he mouthed.

"Bzzt sst sss Bzz," the thing in the grate whispered.

Bud wrote quickly. He sat back. "The Mayflower", he had written. The answer looked right to him. He even remembered hearing it somewhere.

Bud read the next question. He mouthed it at the thing in the grate. He copied the answer as fast as the thing whispered it to him.

His fingers flew. His mouth flapped. Soon he was at the final question.

"Who wrote the Declaration of Independence?" He mouthed.

"Zzzt ss bzzz", the thing in the grate replied.

Bud wrote "Thomas Jefferson" on his paper. He was finished.

Bud looked around the room. The rest of the class was still writing. He raised his hand.

Miss Harrow went to his desk. "My!" she exclaimed in a whisper so she wouldn't disturb the others, "I would never have expected you to be the first one finished." She took Bud's paper back to her desk, nodding approval as she went.

Bud looked up at the grate. The thing in the grate was smiling.

The next day Bud arrived at school early. He slipped into his classroom before anyone else got there. He climbed up on a desk and looked into the grate. It was empty. He frowned.

"Oh, well," he said, "I might as well put this in there anyway." He pulled a bright, shiny red apple from his pocket. He pulled open the grate. He slid the apple inside. He closed the grate.

When the class returned from recess later that morning, Bud looked up at the grate. The apple was gone.

From then on Bud put an apple in the grate each morning. And whenever he was stuck on a question or needed a little help, he asked the thing in the grate. However, just in case the thing might go away and not come back, he always did his homework.

The Monster Maker

"Don't go far," Ernie Cobean's mother said as he headed toward the beach from the family cottage. "And don't go into the water above your knees."

Ernie frowned. "O.K., Mom," he called back.

It was a lovely day. Ernie's family rented a cottage by the sea every year. Ernie loved it by the sea. As he ambled over the sand dunes toward the beach he whistled a happy song. He had a whole week of vacation to enjoy.

Ernie stopped at the top of a high dune. The ocean stretched to the horizon. A ship sailed far out to sea. A few sailboats skimmed the water closer to shore. It was still early morning. There was nobody on the beach yet.

Ernie's frown returned. That was the only problem. He would like to have a friend or two to play with.

"Oh, well," Ernie sighed, "Maybe somebody will show up later."

He headed toward the refreshment stand which was just opening. It served the sunbathers and swimmers who would be coming to the beach during the day.

"May I have a glass of water?" Ernie asked the man behind the counter. The man was busy cleaning the place.

"I don't have time to give water to every kid who asks," the man replied gruffly.

Ernie stepped back. "I'm sorry," he said. He reached into his pocket. "Er, then may I have an orange soda?"

The man turned to Ernie. "Look, kid. I've got to get this place ready for business. I've got customers coming." He pointed to a red, white and blue soda machine. "Get yourself a soda out of the machine. That's what it's for."

Ernie swallowed hard. He had really wanted a friend. somebody he could talk to. Instead he felt more alone than ever.

The soda machine was next to the refreshment stand. Ernie dug into his pocket. He found a coin. It was a shiny quarter. It was all he had. He put the quarter into the machine. He waited for the whirring and clunking. He waited for his can of soda to appear. But the machine didn't whir and clunk. It didn't spit a can out either. The machine didn't do anything. It just ate his quarter and sat there with a stupid look.

Ernie shook the machine gently. Nothing happened. He nudged it hard with his elbow. Still nothing happened. Finally, he was so frustrated he kicked the machine.

"Hey! Cut that out, kid! Don't kick my machine!" the man in the refreshment stand leaned over the counter and shook a fist at Ernie.

"But I . . ."

"Don't give me any buts. Get away from my machine."

Ernie backed away.

"I lost my quarter in it . . ."

The man leaned out of the stand farther. "Did you hear what I said? Get away from my machine!" He shook his fist.

"Get away from my stand. I've got customers coming."

"But I'm a customer . . ."

The man leered an ugly smile. "Let's see your money."

Ernie shuffled back and forth on his bare feet. He dug in the pocket of his shorts. They were empty. "I had a quarter but the machine . . . "

"Sure, sure," the man sneered, "You put it in the machine and didn't get anything."

Ernie smiled. "That's right. That's exactly what happened . . . "

"Get out of here, kid, that's what they all say."

Ernie trudged down the beach. He felt just awful. He was lonely. He was sad. And he had lost his quarter to the stupid machine. He turned his head back toward the booth. "If I had another quarter I wouldn't spend it in your dumb stand, anyway," he said. He dragged his feet through the sand. He felt less and less like going to the beach.

Ernie's head was hanging low. His toes curled over shiny shells and rocks as he walked along the water's edge. He didn't bother to pick them up the way he usually did. He didn't feel like skipping flat stones on the wave tops. He really felt rotten.

His foot stubbed against something soft. Ernie stopped. A lump of gray-green clay the size of a blobby football had washed up on the beach. It was right at the edge of the water. Each wave which came in splashed it and kept it wet. Ernie pressed his toe into the clay. It was firm but soft enough to dig in. It wasn't gooey. It wasn't hard. It was just right for making into a ball.

Ernie dug a handful of the clay from the lump. He molded it into a ball. It was interesting clay, much neater than the stuff he'd used at school. He sat down on the wet sand next to the lump. His loneliness began to pass away.

Ernie rolled the ball into a cylinder. Then he rolled it into a rope. He wadded the rope back into a ball. "What should I make?" he asked himself. He tossed the wad of clay from one hand to another. "I've got it!" he said. "I'll make a whale."

Ernie's fingers molded the clay. But he wasn't very good at it. The whale he made looked more like a midget baseball bat. He mashed it into a ball again. "I'm no good at this," he said. He was going to toss the ball of clay into the sea when he looked at it closely. He grinned. He had pressed a weird sort of face into the clay without knowing it. He forgot about not being very good at molding clay and just let his fingers do what they felt like doing.

Soon Ernie had formed an odd, two-legged figure. It had a head, two arms and two legs, but it didn't look exactly like a person. Ernie pressed little wads of clay into the figure here and there. He made the figure's head very large. He gave it long, thick arms and short thick legs. He molded huge hands the size of a gorilla's. He gave it square feet with no toes. He found a piece of driftwood which he used to model a huge open mouth and a single, immense round eye in the figure's forehead.

Ernie was laughing. It was fun to make a figure and it was even more fun to make it look like whatever he wanted. He pressed some fuzzy seaweed into the clay head and made it look like hair. He rubbed sand into it, covering it completely, so that it looked as if the figure had coarse, tough skin. He put a glistening seashell in the eyehole which stared back like a small searchlight. He molded the fingers into claws. For teeth he gave the little creature two rows of pointed stones which looked like shark's teeth.

When Ernie was finished with the creature he roared. It was the neatest looking thing he had ever made. It was almost as long as his forearm. Standing next to it, the creature came up to Ernie's knee. Ernie sat back down. He stared at the little creature. He scratched his head. He looked at the original ball of clay which had washed in from the sea. He had used no more than a handful of clay. Yet the creature was much larger than a single handful. It would take ten handsful to make another.

"It looks bigger," Ernie said.

His eyes bugged open. He stared at the creature standing on the sand in front of where he squatted. The creature *was growing!* It inched higher and higher.

Ernie jumped back. He was on his knees looking at the peculiar thing. It grew taller and thicker and stronger. Soon it was as tall as he was. He leaped to his feet. The creature continued to grow. In minutes it was as tall as he was, standing up!

Ernie's throat became dry. He turned in every direction. There was still nobody else on the beach. The creature began to wiggle its hands. It began to flex its legs. It began to roll its head from side to side as if it were waking up. It began to blink its eye and gnash its teeth.

"Grrrlllllllwwwrrrrr".

A raspy sound came from the creature's throat.

Goosebumps covered Ernie's arms and legs. He tried to move his feet. He wanted them to run. But they would not obey him.

"Run!" he shouted. "*Please* run."

He was talking to his feet. But to his complete surprise the creature began to run. Ernie stood as still as a statue. The creature bounded down the beach like an overweight wrestler trying to run a dash. Its huge feet thudded wetly into the sand. It made holes a foot deep in the wet sand. And it was still growing.

Ernie watched the thing lumber away. He wiped his eyes. He blinked them. It was true. The little creature he had molded from the interesting clay had actually grown. It had actually come to life. And more marvelous than anything, it obeyed him!

"Stop!" Ernie shouted.

The creature stopped as if it had run into an invisible wall.

"Turn around!" Ernie commanded.

The creature turned slowly like a huge derrick. It was almost like slow motion.

"Come back," Ernie said. He was a little unsure of this last command. What would he do if the thing did come back?

Like an obedient puppy, the thing lumbered back to where Ernie stood.

"Stop," Ernie said.

The thing stopped.

Ernie played with the thing for a long, long time. He got it to do tricks. He had it chase sticks. He could make it roll over. He could even make the creature carry him around on his back.

"Yippee!" Ernie shouted, holding on for dear life as the creature bounded like a wounded buffalo over the sandy beach. It was better than having a horse because when Ernie lost his balance and tumbled off, the thing caught him before he hit the ground.

"Put me down," Ernie commanded. The creature set him gently on the sand.

Clouds began rolling in from the sea. It was soon overcast. Nobody would be coming to the beach. Ernie had it all to himself. He and his marvelous thing would be undiscovered.

Suddenly Ernie had an idea. He wasn't alone on the beach after all. He turned slowly. Far off, no larger than a speck, was the refreshment stand.

"I'm thirsty," Ernie said with a mischievous smile.

In moments he was riding like the wind on the back of his stumbling thing. They would reach the refreshment stand in no time at all.

"Stay here," Ernie told the thing. He pointed to a place behind the refreshment stand where the man wouldn't see him. Ernie walked around to the front.

"Excuse me," Ernie said.

"Oh, it's you again," the man snarled.

"I lost a quarter in the machine before," Ernie said. "It's the only money I've got with me. May I have it back so I can buy a soda?"

The man ignored Ernie.

"May I have my quarter back?" Ernie asked again.

The man snapped at him. "No you may not have your quarter back because I don't believe you put a quarter into the machine. Now get out of here."

"May I try to get my quarter back by myself?" Ernie asked politely.

"Look, kid. I don't believe you put a quarter in my machine. But if that's what it'll take to get you out of my hair, then go ahead." Then the man sneered a really ugly sneer. "But don't you dare touch my machine or I'll fix you good. Haw haw haw!" The man laughed a devilish laugh. "I'd like to see you get your quarter back without touching my machine . . . haw haw haw." He roared at his sick joke.

Ernie grinned. "Thank you," he said.

The man looked at him strangely.

"Thing," Ernie called, "Come here."

The refreshment stand quaked.

The thing thumped out from behind the stand on his short, thick, scaly green legs.

The man behind the counter turned white.

"Get my quarter back," Ernie commanded, pointing at the red, white and blue soda machine.

The thing stepped to the machine. It picked it up in its arms as if it were a cardboard box. It threw the machine to the ground. The machine popped every seam.

The thing kicked the machine a solid whomp. The glass door on the machine flew into space. The thing crashed a huge fist onto the machine. A dozen cans of soda spewed out into the air like a flying parade. The thing jumped up and down on the machine until it was flatter than the Sunday paper. Then it picked up what was left of the machine and tore it in half like it was a thin sheet of tissue. Ernie's quarter popped out onto the sand.

Ernie picked up the quarter and brushed it off. He polished it on his shorts. He walked to the counter. "I'd like an orange soda, please," he said. He put the shiny quarter on the counter.

The man's eyes were bugged open wide. His mouth was hanging open like a sock drawer. His arms fluttered at his sides. He couldn't move. He couldn't speak. All he could do was go, "AaaaAAAaaaAAAAAAaaaaaAAA!"

"May I get my own soda?" Ernie asked politely.

The man only answered "AaaaAAAAAaaaaaAAAAA!"

"Get me a soda," Ernie said to his thing.

The thing walked through the wall of the refreshment stand. It pulled the door off the cooler and took an orange soda. It put it on the counter. Then it walked through the opposite wall. The wind blew in on the stunned man from three ways.

"Thank you," Ernie said to the thing. He put his quarter on the counter and walked away.

Clouds filled the sky. The wind began to blow. Ernie and the thing walked quickly toward Ernie's cottage. It was still far off.

"Just think of the great things I could do," Ernie thought aloud. "I could use my monster to make everything that's wrong right again. The police could use it to stop crime. The army could use it to stop war. It could do the dangerous things people have to do and nobody would get hurt. Gosh!" he exclaimed as he thought of all the good he could do in the world with his marvelous thing, "I could use it to make up for all the awful things people have done to one another. People wouldn't dare be bad any more if the thing were watching . . ."

A drop of rain fell on Ernie's arm. Then another. He looked up into the sky. It was starting to rain for sure.

He looked at the thing. "Come on, we've got to get home before we're soaked," he said. Ernie stopped as if he'd seen a ghost.

The thing stopped too. The rain was falling on both of them. It was raining hard. It was fresh, clear water from the sky. Quite different from sea water. Ernie stared at his marvelous creation. It was melting in front of his very eyes. The rainwater poured off the huge arms and legs. It washed away the seaweed fur. The head began to turn into a blob.

Within minutes the thing was completely gone. There wasn't even a stain left in the sand.

Ernie ran to the edge of the sea where he had found the blob of clay. It too was melting. Before he could grab a handful, it vanished.

The rain began to let up. The black clouds opened up and bright sun poured down onto the beach. A few people arrived. Soon they were followed by others. The sun was warm. The beach would be crowded.

Ernie looked sadly out to sea. "Thank you, Thing," he said. "I'm sorry I didn't get to know you better. We could have done some really great things together."

He turned to leave. He stopped. He looked at the horizon again. The ships and sailboats were still there. "If you ever decide to come back" he said, "I'll be here. Next summer. O.K.?"

A particularly large wave crashed against the shore. It roared loudly and then the sea was calm. Ernie smiled. He finished his soda. "And thanks again for getting me the soda," he grinned.

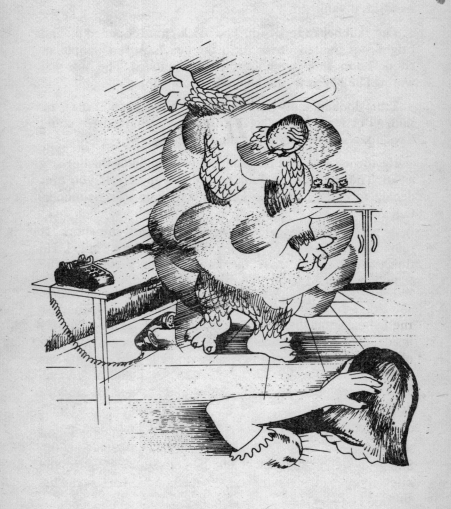

Let It Ring

Mrs. Daniel smiled at Sue Bell. "Billy is already asleep in his room. There are snacks in the refrigerator. Mr. Daniel and I will return about midnight." She stepped out the door. "And, of course, if you need us, just phone."

Sue Bell watched the Daniels drive away. When they were gone she closed and locked the door. She liked baby-sitting, but she felt better with the doors locked. She also liked the lights on. She went from room to room and turned on the lights. Soon the the Daniels' house was as bright as day inside. She went upstairs to Billy Daniel's room. The 5 year old was sleeping. Sue would have an easy job tonight. She smiled. "Thank goodness," she whispered, "He can be such a terror sometimes." She closed Billy's door and went downstairs.

The moment she settled herself in front of the television set the phone rang. She looked at her watch. It was 9:00. She frowned. "Oh, well," she said as she walked to the kitchen where the phone was, "I'll just have to miss the beginning of the movie."

The kitchen smelled of fresh baking. Sue grinned. She knew there was a plate of cookies in the refrigerator for her.

"Hello? Daniels' residence," Sue spoke softly into the

phone. She didn't want Billy to hear her voice. He would come downstairs for sure.

There was nobody on the line.

"Hello?" Sue said, just a little bit louder.

Still there was no answer.

Bzzzzzzz. The line began to buzz.

Sue shrugged her shoulders. She knew the buzz meant there was nobody on the line.

She stopped at the refrigerator. The cookies were there just as she expected. She took one and nibbled it as she headed for the family room.

Bbbbbrrrrrrriiiiinnnnnnng!

"Oooof!" Sue exclaimed as the phone rang again. She hadn't even made it out of the kitchen.

"Daniels' residence," she said.

Bzzzzzz.

She looked at the phone. It upset her. She hung it up. She finished her cookie as she hurried back to the family room. She was missing the beginning of the movie. She wasn't really enjoying the cookie. And she was very curious as to who was calling and then hanging up.

BBBBBBBBrriiinnnnnng!

"Oh! This is going too far!," Sue said as she stomped through the house to the phone.

' "Hello!" she said. She spoke in a normal voice. She was just upset enough not to care if Billy woke up or not.

Bzzzzzzzz.

"Well, if this is somebody's kind of stupid joke I'll . . . I'll . ." she hung up the phone, not knowing what she would do.

As she reached the kitchen door she stopped. The house was very, very quiet. It was pitch black outside. The street passing the house was a dead-end street. There were no cars on it. But she listened. She heard a sound.

Bzzzzzzz.

She cocked her head.

Bzzzzzzz.

She looked at the phone.

"Didn't I hang it up right?" she asked herself.

She went back to the phone. She jiggled it on the hook.

"There," she said, and walked quickly to the door.

Bzzzzzzz.

She stopped. She swallowed hard. Something strange was going on. She felt cold. She turned slowly. The phone was on the hook. There was no question about that. But it was still buzzing.

Sue circled the room. She listened at the door, at the windows, and by the refrigerator. She listened by the sink and by the basement door. Each of these was as quiet as a grave. The only sound she could hear was the buzzing. She put her ear close to the phone.

The buzzing came from the phone.

Goose bumps appeared on her arms.

Sue reached for the phone. She hesitated. Her hand was shaking. Finally she got up her nerve. She put the phone to her ear.

Bzzzzzzzzzz.

She slammed it down on the hook.

Bzzzzzzzzzz.

She covered her ears.

The sound stopped.

She uncovered her ears.

Bzzzzzzzzzzz.

The sound was coming from the phone.

She was growing frightened. Then she smiled. There was another phone in the Daniels' bedroom.

"Oh, you silly goose," she said. "The other phone is off the hook."

Sue went quickly up the stairs. She entered the Daniels' bedroom. She stopped as if the door had slammed in her face. The phone was on its hook. But it wasn't buzzing.

Bbbbrrrrriinnnnnnng.

The downstairs phone rang. The upstairs phone didn't. They were on the same line. They each had the same number. The upstairs phone was just an extension.

Sue ran down the stairs. She ran to the kitchen.

Brrrrrriinnnnnng! Bbbbbrrrriinnnnnnng!

Sue snapped the phone off the hook.

"Hello!" she shouted.

Bzzzzzzzzzzz.

She slammed the phone down. It bounced off the hook and fell to the floor.

Bzzzzzzzzzzz.

The buzzing sound was terrible. It was very loud. It grew louder and louder.

Sue stared at the fallen phone. The buzzing noise it made was so loud that the phone was actually vibrating. She didn't dare move.

42

Suddenly her breath caught in her throat. Her eyes opened wide. Every muscle in her body became tense. She stared at the phone. A pale mist was flowing from the ear piece. It gathered in a cloud near the kitchen floor.

Sue wanted to run. Her legs were rigid. She couldn't move them.

The mist continued to pour from the phone. It was pale at first. Then it grew thicker and darker. It was greenish-brown. It had a peculiar odor. It smelled like old, wet earth and swamp.

"B . . . . bb . . . Billy . . ." Sue tried to call out for the only person close enough to hear her. Even though he was only 5, he was somebody. But her voice was as thin and weak as a moonbeam.

The mist began to swirl. A cloud formed. It grew thick. Sue could no longer see through it.

"OH!" Sue cried. Her mouth flopped open.

The cloud was slowly taking shape. As the terrified girl watched, the cloud bubbled and grew. It swirled like a miniature whirlwind until it was about 3 feet tall. Then it stopped whirling. Thick arms emerged from the cloud. They were scaly and green. They ended in three-fingered hands. Legs formed at the bottom of the cloud. Three-toed feet wiggled and curled at their ends.

The cloud began to clear. Inside the cloud was a body attached to the scaly green arms and legs.

"EEEEEEEEE!" Sue screamed.

It had a head no bigger than a grapefruit. The head was much, much too small for the body. Two tiny green eyes stared out of the head. A tiny mouth opened and closed. A single, black fang jutted from each side of the little mouth.

BZZZZZZZZZZ.

The creature buzzed loudly.

Sue covered her ears.

BZZZZZZZZ!

She could still hear the terrible sound.

The creature took an unsteady step toward her. Then it took another.

BZZZZZZZZ!

Sue whirled and ran screaming through the house.

BZZZZZZZZ!

The buzzing creature followed her. Its legs were short. It could not run well. It loped and staggered after her.

"HELP! HELP!" Sue screamed. She grabbed the door handle. Her hands were wet with perspiration. She spun and twisted the handle but it would not turn. She pulled. She forgot it was locked.

"Mommmmy!" a frightened voice called.

Sue froze. *"Billy!"* she screamed. She dashed up the stairs.

Billy was standing in his bed. He was crying. The noise and screaming had awakened him. "Mommmmmy!" he cried.

Sue slammed the door to his room. She turned the lock. Billy stopped crying. He smiled. He knew Sue. He was no longer afraid. The room was quiet again.

Sue listened at the door.

Bzzzzzzz.

The buzzing creature from the telephone was thumping up the stairs on its short, three-toed legs.

Sue looked frantically around the room.

"The window!" she shouted.

Sue grabbed Billy and ran to the window. She struggled to open it. It was stuck.

Bam! Bam! Bam!

The creature was pounding on the door.

Sue pounded her hands against the window frame but could not budge it.

Bam! Bam! Bam!

The door to Billy's room shook. Paint chipped and cracks appeared in it. The creature was pounding it to pieces.

BZZZZZZZ.

The buzzing grew louder.

Billy stared at the door. He broke out of Sue's grasp and went to it. He began to turn the lock.

"Somebody wants to get in," he said with a grin.

"NOOOOO! BILLLLLY!"

The door popped open. The tiny-headed green creature was right outside.

"Aaaaaaahhhh!" Billy screamed. He ran back to Sue.

The creature's teeny little eyes flashed. Its odd, very small mouth opened and closed like a fish's. Its short, stumpy legs began to move. It staggered closer and closer to the terrified children.

Bbbbbbrrrrinnnnng.

"Aaaa!" Sue cried. She shook her head to clear it. She had to think of something.

Brrrinnnng.

It was the phone. She had forgotten about the extension.

Sue gripped Billy's hand tightly.

"RUN!" she screamed.

The two flew by the smelly creature. They raced out the door. They dashed across the hall. Sue slammed the door to the Daniels' bedroom behind her. She locked it.

"Don't open it!" she shouted.

Brrrinnnnng.

Sue raced to the phone.

"Hello . . . hello!" she shouted. "Please . . . help us . . . there's a monster after us. . . ."

She stopped. Her face turned as white as snow. She held the phone in front of her face. She stared at it.

Bzzzzzzzzzz.

"NOOOOO!" she screamed. She dropped the phone.

BZZZZZZZ. The extension phone was buzzing.

BAM! BAM! BAM!

The creature outside was pounding on the door. It would give way in a moment.

SCRATTTCCCCHHHH! SCRATTTTTCCCCHHH!

The creature's claws scratched at the wooden door.

BAM! BAM! BAM!

Sue wrapped her arms around Billy. She held him close.

The door began to break off its hinges.

The two children were petrified.

BZZZZZZZZ. The extension phone vibrated.

Sue whirled. She stared at the phone lying on the floor. A pale blue mist was seeping from the phone. It swirled into

46

a thick blue cloud. Stumpy, three-clawed arms stuck out from the swirling cloud. Short, three-toed feet appeared at the bottom of the cloud. The cloud stopped swirling. It cleared away. Standing on the carpet 6 feet away from the shivering, whimpering children was a blue creature with a tiny head. Red fangs hung like awful icicles from its teeny mouth.

BAM! BAM! CRASH!

The bedroom door flew off its hinges.

The green creature lifted one leg. It was going to enter the room. Its tiny green eyes blinked. It saw the blue creature.

"EEEEEEEEE!" the green creature shrieked.

The little blue monster shook its scaly, three-clawed fist at the green creature.

The green creature froze in its tracks. It raised its stumpy little arms. It put its three-clawed hands to the sides of its tiny head. It covered its miniature ears.

The blue creature stomped across the room. It reached out for the green creature.

"EEEEEEE!" the green creature cried out.

The blue creature grabbed the green creature's ear and twisted.

"EEEEEEE!" the green creature screamed in pain.

Still twisting hard on the green creature's ear, the blue creature led it across the room past the startled children. The blue creature stopped at the telephone. It pointed to the fallen phone with a pointy claw.

The green creature got down on its hands and knees. It put its tiny little head next to the phone. It began to dissolve. Soon it was nothing more than a swirling mist. It vanished into the phone.

The blue creature put its three-clawed hands on its hips and shook its little bitty head. Then it turned into a swirl of pale blue mist and disappeared into the phone.

Sue and Billy stared at the phone. Billy stepped close. He kicked it with his toe. Nothing happened. Sue picked it up. She put it to her hear.

Bzzzzzzzzz.

She slammed it on the hanger.

The buzzing stopped.

She waited. Then she put the phone back to her ear.

Bzzzzzz.

Was it just the phone buzzing? Or was it something else?

Every time Sue used the phone, she wondered about that.

She would never, never know for sure . . .

Just what IS that buzzing in the phone?

The Mole Monster

"Aaaaaaiiieeee!"

The earth gave way beneath Mike Spence's feet. He felt himself falling, falling, falling. The hole in the ground above his head grew smaller and smaller.

He was swallowed in the darkness of a huge underground cave.

Thrummp!

"Ow!"

Mike rubbed his backside. He shook his head. Everything ached. He was lucky nothing was broken. He looked up. Far, far above his head was a patch of blue. It was the hole. He could see the sky.

Mike hadn't seen the hole. He was on a solo hike. He had packed a knapsack early in the morning. He told his camp leader he would be back late in the afternoon. He set out for Black Rock Forest. Now he was sitting on the damp floor of an unknown cave deep beneath the forest. Nobody knew he was there.

Mike felt around for his pack. His fingers closed over his flashlight. He switched it on. A thin beam of light cut through the darkness.

"Oh, man, am I in trouble," he moaned. The cave was immense. He couldn't see all of it. He turned the light off to save his batteries. The silence was scary. Only the sound of dripping water and his own breathing could be heard.

Mike gathered the contents of his spilled pack together. He did it by feel. His lunch was unharmed. His canteen was still full. He already knew his flashlight worked.

His fingers closed over a small box. It was his first aid kit. He grinned. "The kind of first aid I need sure isn't in here," he said. He wished he had a rope ladder. Or a helicopter. The roof of the cave was very, very high.

Mike slipped his pack on his back. He turned the flashlight on for a moment. He studied the cave. Then he turned the light off. He walked carefully through the darkness. He held one hand in front of him.

"RRRRRRRMMMMMMM!"

Mike stopped. Cold sweat beaded on his forehead. His knees began to shake. His teeth began to chatter.

"RRRRRRMMMMM!"

There was something in the cave with him. Mike stood as still as a park statue. He slowly inched the switch of his flashlight to 'on'. The skinny beam of light cut through the darkness.

"Aaaiee!" Mike screamed.

A giant pair of glowing eyes peered back at him through the inky dark.

The light went out.

"RRRRRRMMMMMM!"

The sound was chilling. Whatever it was, it could see and it could make an awful sound.

Mike retraced his steps to where he had fallen. He looked up. The hole was too far away even to hit with a rock. Even if he could, there was nobody up there to see his signal or hear his cries.

"RRRRRMMMM!"

The groaning moan came closer.

Mike switched on the light.

Standing in front of him, close enough to reach out and touch was a giant furry beast. It was taller than Mike's camp leader, Mr. Selznick. The eyes glowed from inside a huge round face. The thing had very short little arms. They were almost lost in the thick fur. It stood on very short legs. The legs were also buried in the thing's fur.

It looked like a monstrous round, furry Muppet. But it wasn't.

The thing had a mouth on it the size of a car door. It opened wide. Glittering teeth reflected the feeble light of Mike's flashlight. The thing roared.

"RRRRRMMMMMM!"

Mike turned off the light.

"THWWWTTTT!"

Something smelly flew by Mike's ear. The thing had spit at him.

"THWWWWT!" Another spit whizzed past Mike's head.

It was the Mole Monster! Every summer at the camp the counselors told stories about a huge, ugly thing that lived under the ground. It had a hole under a rock where it sat waiting for unsuspecting hikers. Everyone laughed at the stories. Everyone believed the stories were made up to frighten the campers. Now Mike knew they were true.

"THWWTTT!" The Mole Monster spit again. Mike ducked to the ground.

Mike quivered. He knew the Mole Monster couldn't see very well in the dark. That's what the stories said, at least. But it had excellent hearing. It also had a perfect sense of smell. It could get around in the dark better than a blind man.

Mike tried to hold his breath. His heart was beating loudly. There was nothing he could do to make that quiet. His pack rattled on his back.

"What'll I do?" Mike thought to himself. "How can I get away from this . . . this thing?"

A chilling thought occurred to him. "How will I get out of here even if I do dodge him for a while?" he thought. "Eventually he'll find me."

Then Mike remembered the stories about the Mole Monster. "If it sits at its hole under a rock, it has to have a way to climb up there!'" Mike was only half relieved. The creature was stirring. It was lumping toward him on its thick, short legs.

Mike made a dash through the dark. He ran smack into the wall of the cave. He fell with a thud. The Mole Monster turned and followed the sound.

Mike slipped out of his pack. "I can't run with this hanging on my back," he thought. He lay the pack on the ground. "No! Wait a minute," he said silently to himself. He reached into the pack and got his canteen. He threw it as hard as he could. It landed with a loud crash far on the other side of the cave.

The Mole Monster stumbled across the cave toward the rattling canteen.

Mike flicked on his flashlight. He shot the beam around

the cave. "The Mole's path!" he almost shouted aloud. A narrow ledge led from the cave floor to a perch high against the ceiling. Mike turned off the light. He ran toward the ledge. He kept the pack in his hand.

The Mole Monster heard him. It saw the light. It stumbled through the dark after the terrified boy.

Mike clambered up the ledge. The Mole Monster reached it too. It knew the ledge perfectly. It climbed quickly.

Mike reached into the pack. He grabbed his bag of sandwiches. He threw it across the cave. The Mole Monster wasn't fooled. It kept climbing. Mike threw his compass. It clattered noisily. The Mole Monster was getting closer.

The pack was empty. Then Mike's fingers closed around the first aid kit. It was hidden in a pocket of the pack. Mike turned on the light. He shined it into the Monster's face. The thing's teeth glistened. Its eyes glared angrily. Its short arms clawed at the boy.

Mike opened the kit. Inside were bandages and tapes and a bottle of antiseptic. He threw these things at the Mole Monster. His fingers closed on three small glass bottles. They were smelling salts. Inside was a pungent smelling chemical. They were used when someone fainted. Mike felt like fainting. Instead, he threw one of the bottles at the monster with all of his might. The bottle shattered against the monster's nose.

"AAARRGGGGHH!" The monster screamed in pain.

Mike pitched another bottle. It exploded with a terrible stench all over the monster.

Mike scrabbled up the ledge. He had only one bottle left. The monster was still coming.

Mike reached the monster's lookout hole. He grabbed for it.

The Mole Monster grabbed for Mike. Its paws gripped Mike's foot. Mike struggled. The Mole Monster was pulling him back down the ledge.

Mike turned the light on. The Mole Monster blinked at the light. Mike wound up with the last bottle. He pitched it as hard and straight as he could. It hit the Mole Monster square on the end of its sensitive nose. The bottle broke. The powerful chemical ran into the monster's nostrils.

"AAAARRRGGGHHH!" it screamed. Its paws clawed at its face. It lost its grip.

Mike watched in horror as the Mole Monster plunged to the cave floor.

Hands reached into the lookout hole and pulled Mike out. It was Mr. Selznick.

Later, after Mr. Selznick and the rest of the camp had covered the Mole Monster's lookout hole with a huge pile of rocks and had plugged the hole Mike had fallen through with a jumble of logs, they all put their ears to the ground.

"RRRRRMMMMM!"

"He's still there!" Mike exclaimed.

And he is, to this very day.

Monster's Revenge

"We were fools to come on this ridiculous wild goose chase," Professor Douglas Riggs grumbled.

The professor was sitting on the deck of a small boat. He looked over the side. The deep, dark waters of Loch Ness bubbled past the slowly drifting boat.

There's no monster down there," Professor Riggs said, "And anyone who says so is a fool."

Ivan McTavish perked up his ears. He was hired by the expedition leader as a guide. He had lived on the shores of Loch Ness all of his life. He had seen Nessie, as the giant creature which lived in the icy lake was called. More than once.

"Don't be so quick to call a body a fool," McTavish said. "I have seen her," he said proudly.

"Pshaw!" the Professor responded.

McTavish's face turned dark. "Tis true," he said. "Many times."

Riggs got up. He was stiff from sitting. His eyes hurt from staring at the dark water. "Well, where is this so-called monster now?" he asked. He was very, very skeptical. In fact, he didn't believe for a moment there was such a thing.

McTavish cocked his head. He lit his pipe. He watched the smoke drift lazily over the stern. "She's like the smoke," he said. "She's here and there and everywhere."

"Pshaw!" Professor Riggs replied. It was his favorite expression.

They docked the boat at the end of the day. The crew stayed on board. The scientists got off. Professor Riggs jumped ashore.

"I've got a mind to call off this silliness," he said. He had an eye on McTavish. "If it weren't for idiotic stories from the likes of you," he said, "Scientists wouldn't have to chase around the ends of the earth looking for things which *do not exist!*"

McTavish felt his face turn red. He held his tongue.

That night at the Nessie Tavern the scientists were having supper. McTavish sat at the table with them. The scientists were discussing what to do next. Two weeks of investigations had yielded nothing.

"Give her time," McTavish said. "She's out there. Just give her time to get to know you."

"Pshaw!"

McTavish looked across at Professor Riggs. He pointed the stem of his pipe at the snooty scientist.

"Aye, you too, Riggs. Give her time. She may get to like even the likes of you."

Riggs slammed his hand on the table. People eating supper way across the room turned at the sudden sound.

"Nonsense!" Riggs shouted. "I've had enough. I am calling my university tonight. The expedition will be called off by tomorrow."

McTavish sucked on his old pipe. "Have it your way, Professor. But if you want to see the monster, you've got to trust her."

Riggs leaped to his feet. "I've had enough blind trust." he shouted. The people at the end of the room turned to listen. "I trusted you," he yelled at McTavish, "and what has it gotten me? Nothing! I think you have duped my university into spending a fortune on a wild goose chase."

McTavish became as red as the plaid shirt he wore.

"Are you calling me a liar?" he demanded.

Riggs smiled devilishly. "I am calling you a liar." he said. "You have arranged to have this expedition come here so you could be paid as a guide."

McTavish leaped to his feet, twice as high as the Professor had. "I demand you take that back," he shouted. "'Tis a bald lie. I am an honest man. I have never told an untruth in my life."

McTavish stormed around the table. The other scientists were embarrassed by Riggs' behavior. They did not feel they had been lied to. They were honest men. They were looking for proof that Nessie existed. Until they could prove the lake creature did or did not exist, they made no judgment.

"You have called me a liar in front of my friends," McTavish went on, growing angrier, "And you have called me a liar in front of these gentlemen whom I respect and who respect me. I demand that you apologize."

Riggs smiled. He pointed a butter knife at McTavish. "I will apologize to you, sir, when Nessie, your famous "monster" asks me to. Ho ho ho!" He broke into uproarious laughter.

None of the others laughed.

McTavish stared at the crowing man. "You have made a terrible mistake, Professor. But you shall get what you ask."

With that he turned on his heels and left the room.

It was no longer possible to keep the expedition in order. Riggs had made things too uncomfortable. And he had called his university to say that the whole thing was a hoax. He blamed it on McTavish.

By week's end the expedition had left. Nothing remained. The scientists had all left Scotland for their own countries. Riggs had returned to New York City.

"Nessie? I've not asked for favors from you," Ivan McTavish said softly from the stern of his rowboat in the middle of Loch Ness. "I've done my best to find you so others could see you, but I've never tried to trick you or harm you." The night was dark. A sliver of the moon and thousands of stars glowed in the sky. McTavish puffed on his pipe.

"Now I've been called a liar in front of my own friends. I'm askin' you to help me," he said.

The lake began to boil. Huge bubbles burst to the surface. The small boat began to bob. McTavish held on for dear life.

Suddenly a broad sloping back emerged from the depths. It looked like a huge black boulder, as smooth as a polished pebble. McTavish clenched his pipe between his teeth.

Nessie exploded from the inky water. Her long neck reached high into the sky. It arched gracefully above the bobbing boat. Her head, as large as an automobile loomed above the Scotsman like a giant globe. Her eyes were dark brown. Her mouth was closed.

"Nessie!"

The creature lifted itself from the water as high as it could. It was ten times larger than the boat, perhaps more. The slowly curving back continued to glide out of the water. She was larger than a trailer truck. Still the immense mountain of flesh poured out of the deep. The creature was as large as a house.

The thin line of Nessie's lips opened. "Aaarroooowww!" Her mouth was huge. Four rows of glistening teeth sparkled in the pale moonlight, two on top and two on the bottom. A tongue as thick as a fence post darted from her mouth. It was as sharp as a sword. The tongue lashed the air. Fwooosh! Fwooosh!

McTavish ducked to avoid the slashing tongue.

"Then you'll help me?"

Nessie opened her gaping jaws wider.

"AAAARRROOOOWWW!'"

McTavish rowed like a demon. His small boat cut through the water. He reached the end of the lake. A narrow channel at the end of the lake reached into the sea. The channel was too shallow for Nessie. That is why she always remained in the lake.

McTavish unrolled a piece of canvas lying on the bottom of his boat. Inside was a bundle of bright red cylinders.

"Dynamite, Nessie. You've got to get back when she blows."

McTavish placed the dynamite on the channel bottom. The timer was set for 5 minutes. He leaped for his oars and rowed toward the center of the lake. Nessie cruised right behind. She was not even going half speed.

Kaaaaabwwoooooooom!

60

A fierce explosion ripped the air. Tons of water cascaded down. Bits of rock and globs of mud flew through the air.

McTavish looked over the edge of the boat. He had been hiding on the bottom. He grinned. A hole the size of a destroyer had been torn in the channel floor.

"Go find him, Nessie," McTavish said. "Make him apologize."

Aaarrrooooowww!

Nessie seemed to grin. Then she headed for the channel and the open sea.

Professor Douglas Riggs pulled his overcoat around his shoulders. A chill wind blew up the East River in New York City. He headed for his office at the university. His office overlooked the river.

Riggs worked all day long. He was writing a paper to disprove the existence of Nessie, the Loch Ness Monster.

"Ho, ho, ho," he gloated, "I would indeed like to see that liar McTavish when he reads this in the newspapers." He put a few finishing touches on his paper. It was late in the evening. He yawned. He put his head down on his arms. Soon he was asleep.

Arrrrooooo!

Riggs grumbled in his sleep.

Arooo!

Riggs wriggled uncomfortably.

ARRRROOOOOOO!

Riggs sat bolt upright. The hair on his neck was standing up. Shivers were running up and down his spine. His eyes popped open wide.

Riggs reached for the lights. Before he could touch the switch something at the window caught his eye. He whirled.

A mouth as big as the front of a train, glistening with four rows of razor sharp teeth was directly outside his window.

"Aaaaaaahhh!" he screamed.

The mouth snapped shut. The windows burst. Glass went flying everywhere. The force of the wind from Nessie's closing jaws had blown in the windows.

ARRRROOOOOOOO!

Riggs froze.

Nessie raised herself up high until her head was above the window ledge. Then she smashed her forehead against the wall. Bricks and plaster went flying. The wall crumbled. The floor sagged. Riggs' desk glided across the room toward the open wall. Outside was Nessie's open mouth. The desk fell in.

Chlomppff.

The desk vanished.

The floor sagged more. Riggs felt himself slipping. He grabbed the coat rack. It slipped by and fell into the huge mouth and was snapped like a toothpick. His coat vanished as well.

Riggs dug his nails into the wood floor. He slid slowly down the sloping floor. Nessie's hot breath billowed over him.

"Helllllp!" Riggs screamed. But it was late at night and there was nobody around.

Riggs turned. Nessie's slashing tongue ripped the air above him.

Zzzzzztttttt. Zzzzzzttttt.

Riggs pressed his head to the floor. He clawed with his hands. Nothing could keep him from sliding slowly toward Nessie's mouth.

The telephone clattered across the floor. Riggs grabbed it as it went by. He was only a few feet from the desk-swallowing mouth. He dialed 911 frantically. The police emergency operator answered.

"Hellllp!" Riggs screamed. "Help me!"

"What is the nature of the emergency?" the police operator asked.

"A monster!" Riggs screamed. "I'm being attacked by a monster."

"What type of monster is it, sir?" the operator asked.

"Oh, for God's sake," Riggs screamed, "What difference does it make?"

"Please sir, what type of monster is chasing you?"

"It's not chasing me. It's eaten the side of my office. It's eaten my desk. It ate my coat. And now it's going to eat me."

"I understand sir. It's going to eat you. But what kind of monster is it?"

"It's the Loch Ness Monster!" Riggs screamed. It was very hard for him to admit what it was that was waiting for him outside the missing wall of his office. "It's Nessie. The Loch Ness Monster. It's real. It's come to get me.

"We'll send a car over right away sir."

The next morning Riggs' associates snickered among themselves. The morning paper was spread out on the table before them.

"Professor Riggs threatened by Loch Ness Monster," the headlines read. Below, it said that Professor Riggs claimed that Nessie, the Loch Ness Monster, was going to eat him the way it ate his desk.

Riggs sat up in his hospital bed. A group of nurses giggled at him from outside the door.

A doctor scolded them. "Don't tease the man," the doctor said. "He's had a terrible fright. The wall of his office collapsed last night. He believes that Nessie, the Loch Ness Monster did it. Tch tch. He'll never be the same again, of course. Especially now that his fellow scientists laugh whenever they hear his name."

Riggs mumbled. "I'm sorry I called you a liar, McTavish." But nobody heard him. The apology came too late.

On Loch Ness a cold winter wind blew. Ivan McTavish lit his pipe. He looked out over the lake. He grinned. "Perhaps now people will believe me," he said, "Or, maybe they won't. It doesn't make much difference, does it? We know you're real."

He pulled his coat tighter around him. It was a lovely coat. Made in New York.

And by the way, Nessie, m'dear. Thanks for the coat."